Nell's Spells

an

Zip! Zap!

By Katie Dale

Illustrated by
Lindsay Dale-Scott

The Letter L

Trace the lower and upper case letter with a finger. Sound out the letter.

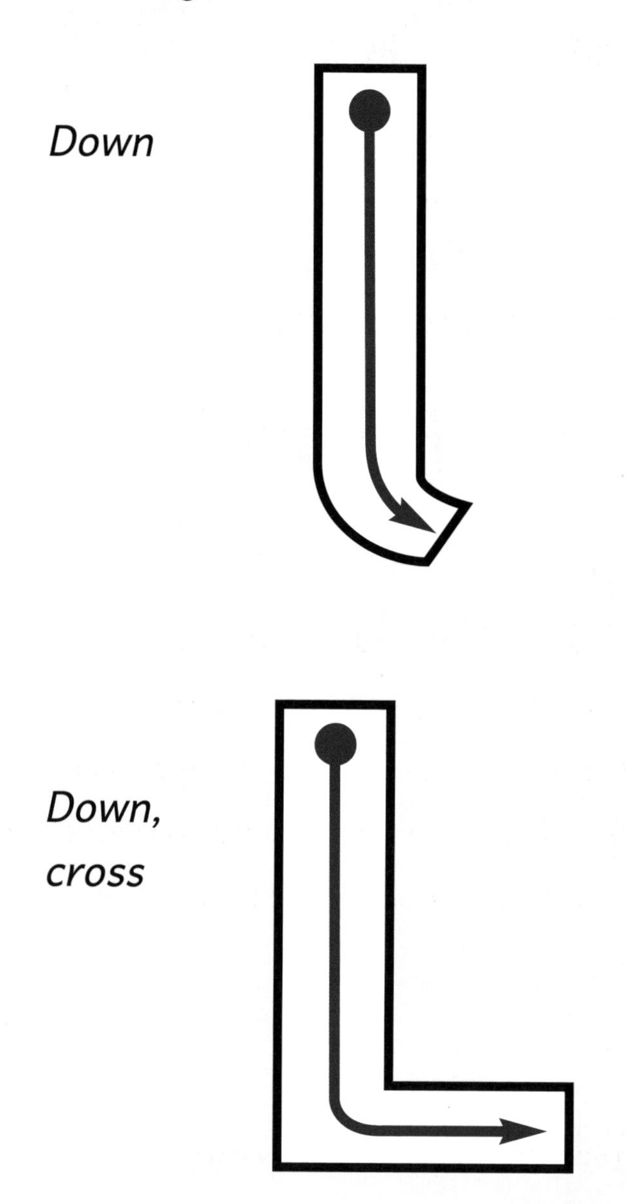

Some words to familiarise:

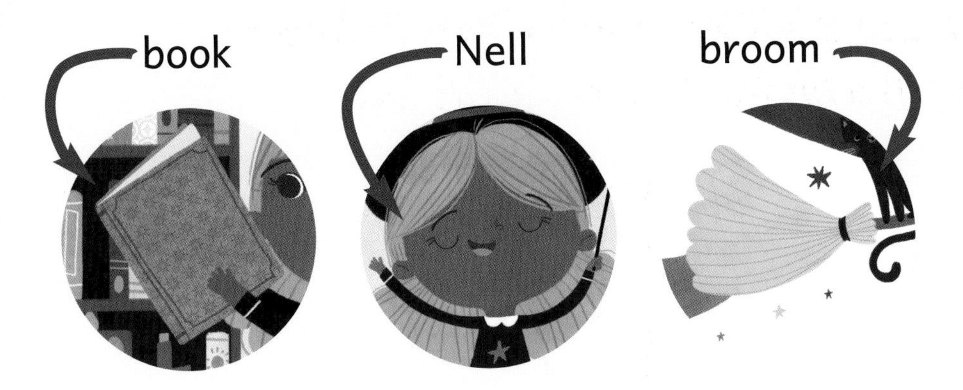

High-frequency words:

a of the put in it

Tips for Reading 'Nell's Spells'

- Practise the words listed above before reading the story.

- If the reader struggles with any of the other words, ask them to look for sounds they know in the word. Encourage them to sound out the words and help them read the words if necessary.

- After reading the story, ask the reader if they remember what Nell put in her pot.

Fun Activity

Can you think of any other spells Nell could cast?

Nell's Spells

Get a hat. Get a bat.

Get a rat. Get a cat.

Get a big fat slug.

Get a big bad bug.

Get a book full of spells.

Get a pot full of smells.

Put the lot in the pot.

Mix it well.

Say a spell.

Get a broom...

ZOOM!

The Letter H

Trace the lower and upper case letter with a finger. Sound out the letter.

Down,
up,
around,
down

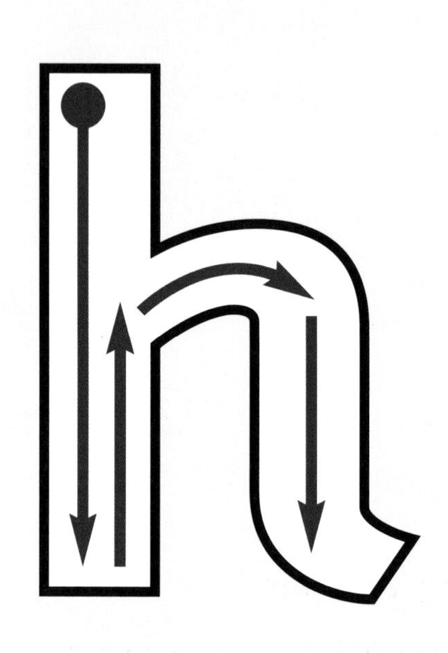

Down,
lift
down,
lift,
cross

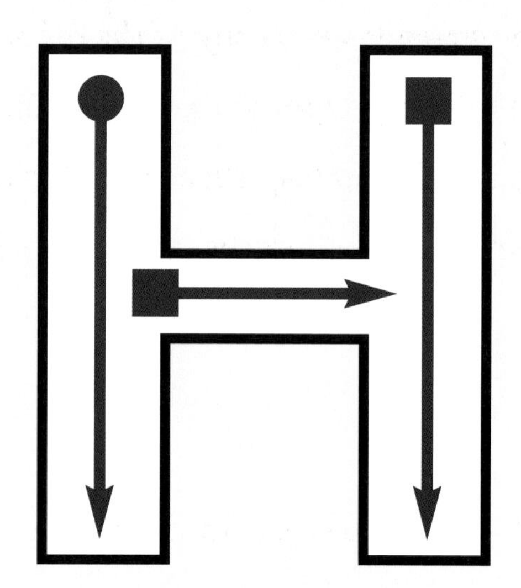

Some words to familiarise:

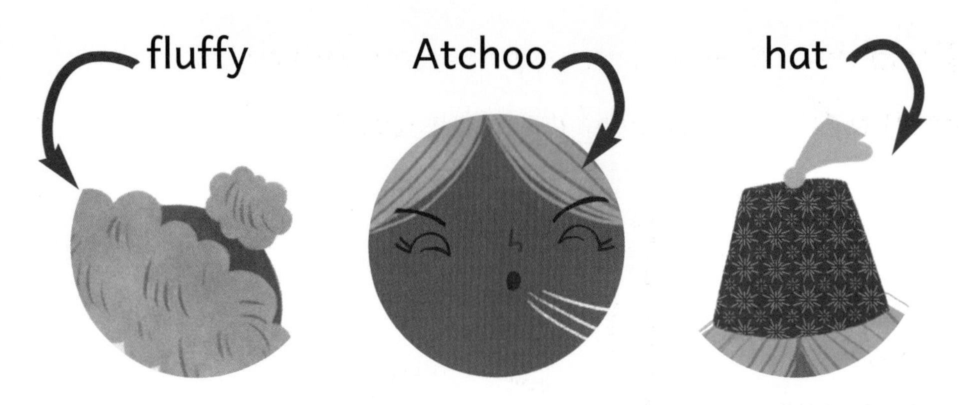

High-frequency words:

is has the her

Tips for Reading 'Zip! Zap!'

- Practise the words listed above before reading the story.

- If the reader struggles with any of the other words, ask them to look for sounds they know in the word. Encourage them to sound out the words and help them read the words if necessary.

- After reading the story, ask the reader which hat Nell thought was best.

Fun Activity

Discuss which hat in the story was your favourite.

Zip! Zap!

Nell has lost her hat.

Zip! Zap!

That hat is too big!

Zip! Zap!

That hat is too fluffy!

Zip! Zap!

That hat is too red!

Zip! Zap!

That hat is too thin!

Zip! Zap!

Yes!

That is the best hat!

Book Bands for Guided Reading

Pink
Red
Yellow
Blue
Green
Orange
Turquoise
Purple
Gold
White

The Institute of Education book banding system is a scale of colours that reflects the various levels of reading difficulty. The bands are assigned by taking into account the content, the language style, the layout and phonics. Word, phrase and sentence level work is also taken into consideration.

Maverick Early Readers are a bright, attractive range of books covering the pink to white bands. All of these books have been book banded for guided reading to the industry standard and edited by a leading educational consultant.

To view the whole Maverick Readers scheme, visit our website at
www.maverickearlyreaders.com

Or scan the QR code above to view our scheme instantly!